Stormborn

Stormborn Saga #1

J.T. Williams

DEDICATION

To exploration, wanderlust, and what could be.

CONTENTS

ACKNOWLEDGMENTS

This novella was the first of an original three book trilogy voted for by and written for the fans of Half-Elf Chronicles. The story has now expanded to over nine full length novels as the adventures of the Stormborn and the crew continue on!

PART ONE: OF EELS AND DWARVES

It was an early morning in the southern Glacial Seas before the sun had risen over the white-capped waves, when to his own desires, a young boy pushed off his blanket and sat up.

He was a determined young man, and though the house was warm and a breakfast was an arm's reach away, he had always felt alone. This was his home, as much as he could call it one. He had no mother and he had no father. He was Valrin, the orphan of eels, or so he had playfully been named now that he spent his mornings gathering them. His Aunt Tua looked after him. She wasn't his true aunt, but he was thankful for her. There were few warm arms to be had in the fishing village of Travaa, and there was even less warmth outside.

Valrin chewed on a fish cake with red berries and strapped up his boots. Donning a slightly bigger-than-needed coat, he slipped on his gloves and pushed open the door.

It was just now entering the months of fall in the southern lands, but the polar lights greeted him. One of his few friends in this desolate port town.

The town itself was built into the rocky shores that went up from a cove that was frequented by fishers in sour weather. The few houses that had sprouted up were generally guest homes used only during the fishing season.

As he went toward the water's edge, he checked two traps for eels. The fishers loved eels and he wasn't too sure why. He never had much luck fishing with them himself but perhaps it was different out at sea. He had never gone fishing on one of the massive ships and actually seen what they used them for. He always hoped to, but he never had a chance.

"Two," he said to himself. "That ought to get me a bit of coffee."

Coffee was a much sought-after substance that Aunt Tua loved. She had looked out for him for as long as he could remember, and she was actually part elven. It got her in trouble by some of the other fishers. The people of the Glacial Seas really sought to keep to themselves and their own races. There were no other elves on the island but she was okay with that. It was strange, in a way, but her careful watch always made Valrin feel like something was different about him. For a while, the fishers said he was good luck. There was even a rumor he had washed ashore during a horrible storm and was chosen by the storm itself to live. Aunt Tua was never very specific on how he came to be.

For years, he heard the names "Storm Child" and "Ocean Soul," but he never felt offended by them. He loved the ocean and storms. As powerful as they could be they made him feel truly alive. As he grew older and now edged toward the years of being a man, by the standard, there were even more peculiar looks at him.

As the sun began to rise, he passed one of the fishers who was much older than the rest.

"Valrin, have you gotten any of your slimy bastards?"

He nodded. "Yes, sir, I do. Were you needing one?"

"Nope, but I have a feeling you will have some traders coming in. I'm going to go fish myself. There are dwarven vessels on the horizon. You know they always bring good wares."

Dwarves were the best for the oddities, and Valrin pranced up the hill to where he could see the other side of the island and the approaching ships. There were several in the outline of the orange sky. He quickly ran to his other traps and began to sack his catches. Running from one part of the island to the other, he went to every nook he'd hid his traps. The people of the village cared little to search for eels themselves. Besides, why do it when they could have a young boy like Valrin do it?

As he returned to his house, Aunt Tua looked him up and down.

"Now you're looking a mess this 'morn."

"I am. Thank you for the fish cakes. You know how much I love them."

"That I do. I was feeling a bit restless last night. I couldn't concentrate. I will be happy when the dark winter comes. Did the other fisher leave out like she said?"

"She did. Her boat is gone."

For the past few weeks, Valrin had spent his days with an elven minstrel fisher named Evia. It was a strange combination, a minstrel fisher, and she was a rare sight. A woman of younger years, and one who took a liking to Valrin.

"Vals," she would say, "you mustn't worry about what others do unless it is their actions that cause harm. Then you must deal with them."

Valrin remembered this and kept it in his mind. He had heard many sayings of the wise, but this one made sense to him more than any. He had seen many misgivings in the port. He had even seen men killed over money.

There was much evil in the world, and he could only do so much to not be saddened by it.

Though Aunt Tua would had rather he waited until they had settled in, it was clear the dwarven vessel he had seen at sunrise was approaching the wooden docks. He quickly carried his simple creatures to see what the dwarves would trade. He knew Aunt Tua wouldn't mind. She stayed indoors during the day and always told him she loved the night, and though it was strange to many, he understood it. As he came near the docks, he noticed this was no fishing ship as he had seen before.

It was a large ship, with green rails and massive pointed crossbows along its deck.

Many stocky dwarves stomped down a gangplank, and a few of them had blood on them.

There was one man who stood in front of them. Valrin didn't like the look of him. He seemed to like bones and was not afraid to shake some poor sea creature's skull at the fishers who had come to greet him.

"I say to you all," he began, "I am a simple dwarf. I only seek a dangerous man who has thus far evaded my capture. There is a ship. Its center mast is destroyed. It has a rough crew of the most dangerous types. Elves. Men. A woman who casts magic from her hands. We need your help. If you see this ship, if it makes port, with great care, simply cast the contents of the bag in a fire."

He handed the bag to one of the fishers.

"I will personally pay the entire island a sum of one thousand pieces of gold and supplies to last the winter tenfold for the capture of this crew."

"Tenfold?" the man taking the sack asked. "What could a crew do so much as to be worth this kind of reward?"

"Do not worry of it," the dwarf said. "Just know that their captain is dangerous and none of them can be trusted. I had some of my own betray me to him, and I would like to deal with the deserters."

The dwarf smiled, and the others with him laughed as they went back to their ships.

Valrin dropped his bag. The dwarves were already leaving.

The men talked among themselves of the vast reward they had been offered. Whoever these wanted people were, they would not be wanted for long.

Valrin was down for the rest of the day. The dwarves, though of a fleet of many ships, were not interested in trade, and it seemed no other ships would come in. Valrin sat on a bluff overlooking the harbor as the sunset began to fall.

"Aye, I know where the wind does blow,
Over icy waters blue,
Forever wandering the depths,
Of a sailor's life, I wish I knew.

Sunrise high and across the sky,
Sun sinks low and starlight shines.
A long night, winter cold and dark,
The polar lights of godly signs.

Ever a night, I think and wish,
For my parents to come from the sea,
Take me back and teach me why,

I only remember a stormy sky."

Valrin closed his eyes and lay back. He looked up at the sky and thought of the island he had called home for so long. The winds blew over him, and he took a deep breath. He then heard something. Something that seemed frantic in nature.

He looked up to see that a ship was coming into the harbor but not very quickly at all. It had red sails, and a center mast was broken down the center. Men used oars to move the ship onto the shore.

As night began to fall and the sun was just leaving the sky, Valrin jumped up and ran down the bluff to the shoreline.

He wondered if this was the ship. The vessel the dwarves searched for. He was one of many who were now on the shore. There were several crewmembers looking out, and several more looking behind them.

A tall man jumped to shore and immediately put his hands up at the rather rowdy group of islanders.

"I am Edanos of the free vessel *Truest Bliss*. We come with no arms drawn, seeking peace."

One of the fishers stepped forward. Valrin knew him as Guna. In his hand was the sack given to them by the dwarf from before.

"We had heard of a ship. Dwarves are lookin' for you."

The crew of the *Truest Bliss* seemed to become disgruntled. There was a shorter man next to Edanos who whispered up to him. A woman stood to his right and pointed to the tree line, and Edanos looked and seemed to nod in agreeance.

"People of this isle, I do not have the fortune of the dwarf captain, nor do I seek to buy your loyalty. I have a small supply of grain for payment to take one of your tall trees on the bluffs. We will need no assistance in harvesting it, and by morning, or sooner, we will be gone."

Guna drew a small blade, as did other fishers, while a vast majority lifted up an arrangement of spiked hoes and even a gigging stick.

"You will not be going anywhere. You will be staying, and we will have a happy winter courtesy of a dwarf's reward."

The many crew aboard the ship drew back longbows. Valrin noticed they were elves. The shorter man grasped a hammer.

Is he a dwarf? Valrin wondered. He didn't seem to have an issue with this captain.

The woman beside Edanos lifted her hands, and a blast of fire landed just before Guna.

"We may be kind," Edanos said, "but do not threaten my crew, fisher."

"Braei, send the man to the afterlife," the shorter man said. "Archers, prepare to release!"

About that moment, Aunt Tua pushed her way through the crowd.

"What kind of nonsense is happening here?"

she asked.

Guna pointed. "These are wanted men, and a good reward is wanted for their heads."

"And how is a wee man like you going to get that reward with several elven arrows in your chest? Not to mention that war hammer." She turned to the captain. "Your crew is welcome to my house, and ignore these rascals. They are only here for a season. It is just me and the boy Valrin here all the time.

Valrin joined her, and Edanos signaled his crew to stand down. Those fishers gathered seemed to do the same, except for Guna.

Edanos went to Aunt Tua and bowed. "Thank you. I assure you we will be here only as long as necessary."

The fishers all went their own way as the bulk of the ship's crew disembarked. Guna shook his head, obviously disgruntled, but having lost his support, he, too, sank away.

Valrin watched as many elves stood on different parts of the ship. They were tirelessly watching the opening of the cove.

As a large group of the crew, including the one called Braei and the dwarf, went to harvest the tree, the captain was beckoned to Aunt Tua's house.

Valrin was amazed of the man. He had no hair on his face, a strange fact for those of the Glacial Seas. He wore a dark tunic with metal brooches and a curved sword.

"Mr. Edanos, will you sit and have some tea? I

have a large stew I've been cooking and a store of dried meat. If it is not enough for your crew, my apologies. I didn't expect such an arrival this time of year."

"Your kindness is almost overbearing. I will gladly accept, and thank you for your words against the men outside."

She smiled. "They are too simple-minded to even be called men. They are pigs, in truth, and I'm happy when they leave. You have an attractive woman with you. I'd say watch her."

Edanos laughed. "Braei can well take care of herself in an unscrupulous crowd. I promise."

As Valrin stared at the captain, he looked away as he was noticed by Edanos' careful eyes.

"Do you live here, son?"

"I do."

"Your father a fisher?"

"I do not know him. My father and mother were lost to me. I came here in a storm."

Aunt Tua seemed to look at Edanos as he nodded and centered his gaze. "A boy of the storm? There are legends of such boys and girls, at least among the seafaring folk. A lost race of long ago, before the seas covered these lands, was said to bless the realm with certain souls who would be born of storms who had access to the old knowledge. They actually created souls. Can you believe it?"

Valrin nodded but he wasn't actually sure he believed it.

"I have spent much time on the many seas of our lands, but these seas call to me. There is something to be upon these waters with the story I just told you. I, too, have no parents to call my own, but the sea has been good to me. I have great friends, and we do what we can to help those in need. These pirates are the worst kind. They may promise riches, but they will take over your island. You will be taken care of, but only as slaves."

"A bit rough for a young boy to hear?" Aunt Tua said.

"True, but this world is rough. A world full of the coddled is a world in chaos. I find it is better to accept truth as it is."

There was a knock at the door, and Edanos jumped, his hand to the hilt of his blade. Aunt Tua opened the door, and in stepped the short man.

"Looking for our captain," a man said.

"Come on in," she told him. "He is here."

As he stepped into the house, followed by the woman, Aunt Tua beckoned them to sit as well.

"The wood is in place," Braei said. "It will hold until we can get to a proper shipwright. But we should avoid any run-ins until we have a proper job done."

"Aye," the short man said, "and storms, or we'll be fishing our sails out of the seas!"

"Braei, Rortho, this young man is Valrin of the seas."

"Another?" asked Rortho.

Aunt Tua seemed to be more disgruntled. But

Valrin wasn't sure if that was exactly the emotion. She was suddenly more distant than before.

"Yes," Edanos confirmed, "one like me. One destined for the water."

As it was now clear to the others that Aunt Tua was upset, Braei stood to help her serve the food.

"Thank you, ma'am, for the hospitality. The fishers are tending to our other crewman. It seems your words have caused a change of heart from the others here."

"Yes," she said plainly.

She served the food to them and sighed before going towards her room. Valrin was curious of it but then turned to the others as they ate. Edanos took out a ring he kept in one of his pouches. He handed it to Valrin.

"Have you seen one of these?"

Valrin shook his head. The ring had a brilliant speckled white glow in the center of a blue field.

"It allows you to go under the surface of the water but not drown. It is only usable by some. Put it on. Let us see if you possess what I believe you do."

Valrin put on the ring slowly, a bit concerned over what he was actually doing. As the metal rested on his finger, it began to glow slightly.

Edanos smiled. "We are brothers of the same world, Valrin. I'm happy we have met."

It was at that moment that Aunt Tua emerged from her room. She had a single silver chained piece of jewelry in hand. She handed it to Valrin with tears in her eyes. He was confused. He had never seen her so upset, and he was worried of why. As the fire glowed behind her, she sat down at the table.

"I knew at some point the truth would be known, but I did not know it was now."

Edanos sat up in his chair.

"You have only been with me for just over twelve years, but when you came here, I was already older than you may believe. I came to the north for the darkness. I was infected some time ago with a kind of curse that while I received a potential cure, it did not remove my sensitivity to the harsh sun.

"I had prayed to Wura to give me purpose in this desolate place, and that night, you washed ashore with that amulet. I took up my guard of you. I accepted my curse and remained here, watchful. I had a purpose and I rid myself of my cure to assure I could protect you." She gave him the amulet. "I know not what it is, but I do not believe in coincidence. Not anymore, at least. Perhaps this man can tell you more of it. I have a feeling about him."

Edanos leaned in, looking at the amulet in Valrin's hand. He touched it with his hand and then nodded, looking at the boy.

"This is special, something that's a sign of—"

A hurried knock on the door cut off the captain's words. He stood up as Braei made it to the door before anyone else. It was one of the elves.

"Captain! The men are all sick; they put something in our food."

Those within the house stumbled out. Valrin immediately noticed that many of the crew were lying on the ground, grabbing their stomachs. It also seemed that other members of the crew had not eaten, and angrily held their weapons out at the fishers. It was then Valrin looked up to the bluffs. The other fishers had lit a large fire, and a white glowing plume filled the sky over the island.

"It is a signal," Rortho said." They are signaling the fleet."

"Then we must go now," Edanos ordered. Valrin and Aunt Tua stood back as the three sailors moved toward their crew on the ground. Gura stood between them and the sickened crewmembers. A large group of dwarves came from the ship.

"We see our old master coming this way quickly. We must go now."

Edanos drew his curved blade, holding it toward Gura. "I only kill when I must, and this is looking to be a situation that doesn't fair well for you, fisher."

Valrin noticed several ships on the edge of the cove making a slow but deliberate approach. From what he could see in the moonlight, none of these looked exactly like the ship that had been here before.

"Stay, Valrin," Aunt Tua told him.

She began to walk at a hastened pace toward the confrontation between the crew of the *Truest Bliss* and the fishers.

He followed behind, although kept back far enough to hopefully not alert his aunt.

"You can strike me, Captain," Gura said, "but I assure you, you will die by the hands of one of the many on this island."

Aunt Tua walked up to Gura and pushed him in the chest. "You have had good catches this year. The gods have blessed you, and this is how you repay them. By selling out a crew who has not shown any violence to you."

Gura pushed her back and pointed at her face. "You inbred elf, why don't you act normal for once in your life. I should have waited until morning. I wouldn't have to see your scarred face, you filthy bitch. I know who else spends their nights up, but you're not even an ounce as attractive as a harbor wench from a few islands over. You're old, washed out, and weak."

Gura kicked her in the stomach, and she fell to the ground. He spat on her, and then Valrin noticed she was to her feet in a flash, to the utter surprise of the fisher.

"You know not who you speak to, human," she yelled.

It was that moment when from the darkness of the bluff came several figures. Edanos looked up.

"Rugag," he said to the others.

As the figures approached, the captain from

before, Rugag, was clapping.

"Very good, very good. I knew they would come here. I had hoped to get at least some sleep, but we were never too far away."

Rugag went to Gura and handed him a bag of silver.

"A payment on a promise to be had in time. You've done good for your island. It will now be a port for the dwarven lord of Barbs. All upon the island and the waters surrounding it, are now under the protection of His Majesty and all property here is now his."

A sudden grumbling roar came from the other fishers.

"Keep calm, keep calm," he said. He then walked toward Edanos, lifting his ax up as he did.

"Come quietly, you sea wretch. I have enough men to take three dwarves and ten Rusis. I can take you, alone."

Rugag then looked down at Valrin. His eyes widened, and he stepped past Aunt Tua. He pointed a chubby finger at him.

"A Stormborn here? This amulet, it is what we need. Come here, boy!"

Valrin stumbled backward and began to run just to have Rugag grab him.

He began to scream, kicking and punching before taking aim with his fingers and digging into the dwarf's eye. Rugag threw him onto the ground and cursed.

"Damn boy." He lifted his ax up to strike when

Aunt Tua suddenly jumped over Valrin, grabbing the ax, and her face turned white. She let out a blood-curdling scream. Her mouth elongated, and sharp fangs glistened in the moonlight.

"Vampiric bitch!" He punched her in the face, dropping his ax and driving a jagged dagger into her throat.

"Aunt Tua!" Valrin cried.

A blast of magic struck the ground near them, and Valrin felt a hand grab him. He looked up at the deck of the *Truest Bliss*. Elven archers fired into pursuing dwarves as he was carried up the gang plank. Valrin was tossed on to the deck of the ship by Edanos, who then shouted to the crew.

"Cast off! We must go now!"

Braei stood on the plank, helping the few of the crew who could still walk, and pulling another who just happened to be on the ground right near her.

"They're killing the others," Rortho said, tossing two more of the crewmen on the deck.

"We have to raise the sails. The other vessels are upon us," Edanos said.

Braei began to pull up the plank to the ground when several dwarves came upon her. Valrin watched from the railings as she reached out, a blast of fire throwing one back. Another slammed his ax just over her head, and she turned, attempting to pull herself on deck.

One of them grabbed her leg, and in a shrieking flash, Aunt Tua was on them. Her face was covered in blood, and her body had multiple stab wounds.

"Aunt!" he cried out, but she turned her attention to other dwarves.

Rortho pulled Braei up and then the gangplank as the ship began to lurch forward.

"Valrin! Stay down!" Edanos ordered. A series of bolts flew across the deck, and he fell to his stomach, crawling away from the fire that took many elves and men off the deck of the *Truest Bliss*. He had thought of sailing many times, but he never imagined it as this.

From his spot behind a stack of crates, he saw the massive ships on either side of them. Braei ran along one edge of the ship, casting bolts of lightning from her fingertips as ropes with claws came along the railings of the ship. Men cut them and slashed at dwarves who attempted to board them. A loud and harsh horn called from the two ships, and several more dwarves came in waves upon the deck.

Edanos, who had been at the helm of the ship, dropped down to the deck level and began fighting the intruders. In several swathes and parries of his sword, he forced his way along one side, cutting the hold the ship on their right had, before turning to the one on the left.

"Kill them!" Valrin heard shouted from the shore. "Kill them all, except Edanos!"

The wind seemed to increase. The sails of the ship lifted up, and they broke away from the one ship; however, the other ship was still boarding them.

"Their sails!" Rortho shouted. "Take out their sails, Braei!"

The Rusis shot a blast of fire toward the other ship, catching one sail aflame before another crossbow bolt flew into the side of the ship.

Valrin stood up, seeing the tensed rope in the ship. It was just out of range of sword, and it seemed the Rusis was now engaged with two other dwarves. Valrin saw a large spear. He grabbed it and ran to the edge, stabbing the rope, attempting to fray it and break the hold the ship had on them. Smaller bolts began to fly toward him, striking the wood around his head. Dwarves on the ship saw him, and they had no issues with killing someone as young as Vals, especially aboard this ship.

As a massive crank on the ship began to pull the *Truest Bliss* into a fatal position, a screech split the air, and Aunt Tua appeared on the deck of the opposing ship. She tore apart the mechanisms and slashed her clawed hands into the dwarves who faced her. She then jumped onto the rope holding them in place and bit the line. The rope dropped, and she jumped back to the edge of the dwarven vessel. Several ax heads cut into her head, and she fell into the water.

Valrin began to cry.

"Now, lift sails. Let's get out of this place!" Edanos said.

Valrin followed the captain up to the upper deck as they moved with haste out of the cove.

There were many ships on the other side of the island, but in their folly, the dwarves had not expected them to escape. They reached open sea and began heading north, Valrin's home well behind them.

Valrin collapsed on the wooden deck. Edanos gave the wheel over to Rortho. Braei came up to the same area, and he tapped her on the back.

She looked to him. "That was close, Captain. We lost at least thirty men, but—"

He cut her off and dropped down to Valrin. "She was your only family you had known?"

With tears falling down his face, he nodded.

"Do not worry, son. You are with us. Your aunt was a kind woman, and her curse, as she called it, ended up saving your life and the lives of my crew. I, too, was like you with no family. You will call this ship home."

Valrin looked up and forced a small smile.

Edanos pulled him to his feet. "You need rest, and this ship is far from danger, and for now, we can assure you sleep. We can talk more of our futures tomorrow."

Edanos took him to a lower level and a single door with a golden outline around it. This was the captain's quarters.

Valrin looked around at the large collection of books, trinkets, and sea charts like he had only seen in the one time he was allowed on one of the large vessels that came into port.

There were several simple beds with small

windows looking out to the sea.

He sat down on one, and Edanos smiled. "Sleep well, young Valrin. There is much we will speak of tomorrow."

PART 2: AN ANCIENT SECRET

Valrin had never attempted to sleep on a ship at sea. In fact, of the many small boats he had been on in his life, this was the first actual ship he had really spend much time on at all. He awoke to sunlight coming through the window above his head. The rank smell of the wood by his head caused him to curl his nose, and he threw his feet over the edge of the bed. He stood up, surprised he had not awoken earlier, and then immediately thought of his aunt, Tua.

Now he understood why she did not like the light. Why she only was in the dark. She had the blood of a vampire. She had been bitten, and that was what she had run to the north for. He touched the pendant around his neck and exhaled. He was deeply saddened by the events, but there was a curiosity in the air, a feeling under his feet, like there was much more within reach than before.

The ship lurched, and he struggled to stand. His stomach turned and felt queasy.

He needed fresh air. He made his way to a dark wooden door and pushed it open. The blow of a salty but icy breeze hit him, and he looked around to see glaciers. It was very bright outside, too. He recoiled back just as Edanos came around the corner.

"You're going to need a bit more warmth out here than you're used to. The winds of Dimn blow upon us with a howl."

It must have been obvious to the captain that Valrin wasn't feeling well, because as soon as they were back in the captain's quarters, Edanos handed him a jar of crushed herb.

"For the ocean shakes your stomach is having. You will get used to it in time."

Valrin took a few of the leaves and chewed them. They were harshly bitter and sent a tingle to his nose, but in just a few seconds, he was feeling better.

Edanos went to a wooden chest with black brackets and pulled out a large coat.

"It is a bit big for you, but I believe it will work until we can find something better. I can get you something more appropriate soon. Rortho's repairs are holding, but we need to resupply and perhaps find some more men."

"Thank you," Valrin said, "for taking me in."

"Do not thank me. I only did what was right. I know that in time, all of our paths will make more sense. I had thought it was the end of our quest when our center mast was destroyed, but now I have more faith in it overall."

Edanos went to an alcove in the room where a kettle was hung. He touched it with his fingertips. "Good, it's still warm. Do you like coffee?"

He nodded.

After serving two cups of the black brew, Edanos sat down with him.

"What questions do you have for me?" he asked.

Valrin couldn't think of any questions on the fly. He stared at the captain, who drank his coffee and simply waited. He didn't feel rushed; he didn't even feel nervous. This was the first stranger he had felt completely calm with in his entire life.

He took a sip of his coffee. It was a bit bitter but still good. He looked down at the pendant around his neck.

"Storm Children or . . . Stormborn, you say you are one too?"

"Aye, I am. That necklace shows your tie to the sea and passage to a place that, well, you are lucky to be able to go to."

"So you have one too?"

"I did, but it was taken from me when I was very young. You were lucky to be left on an island like you were. I was not so lucky. I ended up on an island of unscrupulous characters and many just simply hoping I was worth something on the market. I spent time as a servant boy, if you can imagine it, and the only valuables I was left with were my hands. I had a few friends, if you could call them that. My necklace went to the king of the Barbs, the dwarf king Rugag spoke of, but he never knew what it was, not yet, at least."

"So they know what it is. They could go to this place, too."

He nodded. "They can. But they cannot find it. There is an old secret, a weapon in both sight and words. It is a powerful object and unlike any other attainment to children such as you and me. It is something that binds to your very life force. It becomes a part of you. I have never seen it, but I know of it."

Valrin laughed. "It sounds like some spiritual thing."

"Yes." He laughed as well. "Something like it, I guess. In the end, my goal has been to get my jewel back. I have traveled over many waters and, for many nights, stared at the stars, looking for my purpose. I have found it, and we will go to a town where there is someone who can help us."

Edanos stood up. "Was there anything else you wondered? You are on a ship for the first time. Do you want to see the rest of the ship, perhaps climb to the crow's nest and see the view?"

Valrin finished his coffee and thought of Edanos' question. He knew what he wanted to do, but he wondered if it was too soon or too forward. It wasn't something the captain had suggested. He stood up and decided to see if it was possible.

"Can I steer the ship?"

The captain smiled. "I would like nothing better."

They exited the Captain's Quarters, and Valrin looked out across the ocean as they ascended the stairwells to the upper deck. The sea was vast and empty, a light blue in all directions, with a bright sun that was floating lower in the sky. Rortho had the helm of the ship and gave it up to Edanos as he approached.

"Valrin, come here."

He went up to the wheel and placed his hands on the wood.

"A ship should be a part of you," Edanos began. "When you feel the rock of the waves and your weight shift from one boot to the next, you enjoy it and imagine the ship as your body and your body upon the sea itself. When you change course, it should feel as if you are simply moving over the surface with ease."

Valrin could feel the tug of the rudder, and then shifted the wheel to his left, sending the ship to his right in a lunge.

"Easy," Edanos told him. "Keep it straight for now."

He shifted the ship back the other way and, this time, did it with grace.

"Good," Edanos said.

He looked down at the crew moving on the deck below. Some worked on ropes, others sharpened spears and swords, while watchers looked out from the deck for other ships.

He then looked up into the sails. They were a mix of patchwork and different colors. The masts had marks from flames, and even a few arrows stuck in parts of the ropes. A flag was at the very top of the masts. It was dark blue with no adornments.

"We fly the flag that is the color of our life-giving force. By our, I mean we, as Stormborn. The ocean is our life. We come from it, and we will, in time, return to it."

Braei, the Rusis woman, joined them now. She came from below decks and held a bag of tobacco.

"We are running out," she said.

She began to scrape out a black pipe before packing the bowl and lighting it with a small firestick from a brazier at the aft of the ship.

"We will get more," said Edanos.

"You take us north. Where might we go to get something like that?"

"Merea," he told her.

She looked at him in surprise that even Valrin noticed as he glanced back.

"Then you have told him? You mean to go through with it?"

"We did not survive the night before to pass on this chance. He knows of the secret. He is excited about it."

Rortho now took out his own pipe. He packed it and began to smoke almost as quickly as he had grabbed the pipe.

"My kin will figure out that we are up to something. Before, we guarded the migrating humpback whales, and now we abruptly go north. He knows you have the amulet."

"I do not have the amulet; the boy does. I will not take from him what is not mine."

"Do you know what power you could give up?" Braei asked.

"No, I do not. Neither do you nor do you know exactly what will happen before we can get there. We will go to Merea and speak with one who can guide us. I know this isn't exactly what we planned, but I need to face that I may never get my own back. The boy came to our lives by the will of the gods. We will not spit upon their workings."

Valrin continued to hold the wheel. It was obvious that the two main crewmembers of the captain were a bit perturbed by his decision involving himself. He didn't understand why, but for now, he knew it wasn't his place.

Though she was a bit abrasive, Braei offered to take him below deck. Rortho took the wheel again, and Edanos was to retire to his cabin for some time. He followed her across the deck and into the belly of the ship.

The crew area was tight quarters compared to that where Valrin had slept.

"Our crew changes frequently. Normally law breakers or some just trying to get away from their problems. We even have dwarves of Rugag. They were left on an island to freeze to death, and while I was okay with it, Edanos seems to not be able to do what is needed."

"Isn't it good he helped them?" Valrin asked.

She laughed uncomfortably. "You are young, innocent in the world. I do not doubt my captain, but I would have left them to die. Dwarves, at least in these parts, are not the type you help. Rortho has been friends with Edanos since Edanos was your age. He is the only dwarf this Rusis trusts."

"What about you? How did you join the crew?"

"I was rescued by him from a southern vessel that came to attempt to find 'exotic' slaves. If you can believe it, even Rugag's fleet helped Edanos in the effort to protect the northern waters. I was very young, and the only memory I have is of men wearing red garbs shouting and dying around me. Edanos pulled me from a cell and said I did not need to fear. That was twelve years ago."

"So how old are you?"

She laughed. "Old enough to tell you that you're asking too many questions now!"

She led him to another area of the ship, walking past many stores of food to an area with an assortment of bladed weapons.

"They may not like it, but you need one. Pick something out; make sure it feels good in your hand."

He looked over the many curved and straight blades of varying lengths. He picked up a sword but found himself unable to lift it. He pushed it back on its side. He then took an ax in hand, but it felt too sloppy.

"I don't know. What would you pick?"

The woman opened her hand, and a small ball of fire illuminated the room. "I need no bladed weapon, but pick one you can at least use and not be tired after your second swing."

He pulled a curved blade, similar to Edanos'.

"A scimitar? That will be tiring. Go with a shorter blade for now, like this one." She pulled a short but polished blade from the rack. "Now, come on, above deck. We will be nearing port soon."

Back topside, he walked along the deck, touching engraved wood and jumping from the snaps of the sails as the winds shifted. The air upon him was like the icy blows of a winter storm, but he felt invigorated. In the distance, he began to see an island.

In time, he went to the front of the ship, staring at the outlines of buildings on a snowy and rocky cliff-side town. The port area of the town was actually under a monstrous overhang of the city itself. Atop the massive cliffs was a snow-covered dome of sorts. As they came underneath the city itself, he noticed that the dome actually had a fire burning within it and suspended gardens just visible from the docks, spiraled vines that had frostbitten ends hanging down the cliffs.

"A wonder of our world," Edanos told him.

"Merea grows food for the many regions of the Glacial Seas. It is a place of both wonder and corruption, but it's a free city and not under the influences of Rugag's types."

"How has it remained unaffected by the Barb king?"

Edanos pointed above them.

"Do you see the red crystals growing out of the rock?"

"I do."

"Those are marvelous dwarven constructs, back when the dwarves of this region were not as they are now. If danger threatens this small town, the weapons activate, and any ship caught in the water meets an untimely fate."

"Have you seen it?"

"No, but the fear of such an action keeps the dwarves far away. We are safe to do our business here, and while the ship is worked on, you and I will go into an older part of the town. Cover your amulet up. We do not want questions before the opportune time."

The ship moved along the dock and was quickly tied off. They stepped off the ship, and Valrin was careful to bind his cloak around him. The docks themselves were made of stone and had runic etchings on the path they walked.

"These docks are actually older than you can imagine. The dwarves simply built their buildings above it. The sea people from before were an ancient race, powerful beyond most magic. Their true culture was lost long ago."

They left the regions of the docks and took a road through tall stone buildings with many people of varying races walking around. Though he had lived his life at sea, Valrin had never seen a person with gills like a fish on their necks.

He tried not to stare, but it was such an odd sight, he couldn't help it.

"They are elves crossed with merpeople. Do not stare—they've been known to ink someone. I understand it is not the least pleasant at all!"

The smell of the salty air was stronger here than the actual sea. Cured fish hung in alleyways that were open to the cold sea breeze. They were walking up a hill, and with each step, Valrin's legs burned. They came to a flat area with many stalls on either side. Edanos went to the stalls and grabbed several different garments, stopping to look at Valrin.

"I think, um, I guess it right."

He paid the stall keeper and gave the clothes to Valrin.

"You can dress properly once we get inside the chapel. The woman we meet will keep us waiting. It is what she does. It will give you time to become more comfortable."

Valrin didn't know where they were going, but he felt that at the very least he would happily put on new clothes.

They began up a narrow stairwell that wrapped up and around a series of buildings that rose up in an almost badly constructed tower. At last, they came to a single double gate and a long pathway that went over the sea. Edanos opened the gate, and they entered. The pathway actually was open to the sea at just past Valrin's hips. He felt nervous, and he even thought he felt a sway to the stone bridge way with the cruel glacial winds.

He bound his coat over his head and watched Edanos' feet to lead his path. They came to a large building with a single crystal atop. It had a window, a lone circular lookout that wrapped around one-half of a crowning tower just off center from the crystal.

Edanos knocked on the door and waited. At least the area they stood in now was shielded from the outside winds.

"Go ahead, change. It will be a moment."

He quickly took off his coat and put on the new clothes bought by Edanos. It felt weird wearing something not made from sheep's wool by his aunt. It fit well, though partially tight along his chest.

"You will get used to it. Floppy clothing makes a poor man. You should look your best, particularly if you are captain of a ship."

Valrin wasn't a captain, but he valued the guidance from his new friend.

"It has been some time since I came here. She will wonder of why I have been away. Let me converse with her before you speak."

The door cracked open.

"Edanos, you leave me alone too long," a voice said.

"I come to see you now."

The door shut. Edanos knocked.

"I am not here. Go away."

He knocked again.

"She is not here. Go away," the same voice said.

"I really must speak with you," he said into the door.

"Did you bring me something?"

"Yes." He shook his head, looking at Valrin. "A new friend."

"Can I eat it?"

Valrin closed his eyes and dropped his head.

"I forgot. She likes a snack. Just, just wait here and don't fall for her crazy stories. She likes to entertain."

Edanos immediately began into a quick jog, and Valrin had no clue where he was going.

"So are you human, I guess? Or elf? I normally can smell elves and holy dwarf dung. I know you're not one of those sea cucumbers. What is your name, Stormborn?"

How does she know that? he wondered. "Valrin."

"A name of importance, like Edanos, but better, stronger. Have you ever been to Merea?"

"Um, no. Never. I came from a small island to the far south."

"I see. The storms of old blew further than that, but many never awake to their paths. It seems you have. There is much to speak of, but I fear that there is not the time for all to be spoken. We will talk again, after our meeting, at a different time. A time when you will wonder why I said this, but fear not. I do not just babble as some might say."

It was a few moments later, and Edanos returned.

"She wasn't babbling on, was she?"

"I told you," she said from the other side of the door. "Do you have it?"

Edanos held a fish in his hand.

"Yes, I have your gift."

The door seemed to creak open, and Edanos straightened the collar of his jacket. "Come on, and don't touch anything," he warned him.

The brightness of the outside was a stark contrast to the shadowy interior Valrin found himself in. It was an entryway with multiple candles in tiny recesses in the wall. There was a circular room sunken into the floor ahead down eight steps. The entire room had water flowing in a circle around the floor even though Valrin looked out the window and could see the expanse of the sea. He had no idea where the water was coming from. There were stone pews in a half moon facing a large statue of a mermaid. A fountain was below the statue's feet, and he heard the voice of the woman again.

"Feel the power of the Storm Children, together, interwoven in fate and action to seek out the one place they both desire for their destined fates so long ago foretold."

"Do you intend to game, or will you show the boy your face?"

"Testy human, we of the merfolk do as we want. Fish. Now."

"You're not a mermaid," he said plainly, tossing the fish into the water.

There was a soft laugh through the halls and the sounds of water rushing to and fro around the room. Valrin noticed the water flowed without sense, moving up and around the room and then back down to the pool before the statue. At last, the water all moved toward the statue, moving up its form and then sticking to the stone itself. The stone seemed to come alive for a moment, its eyes glowing brightly, and then a watery figure stepped into the pool. The fish turned to blood and was absorbed by the entity.

Valrin reached out, and Edanos slapped his hand. "Do not touch the messenger of the god!"

"Let the messenger decide of whom can touch her," the watery form said.

The hand reaching out was just as Valrin's, except there was no bone or flesh, just water. He had retracted his hand, but now he took her beckoning and touched her.

"Of the sea, of the streams, of all that is and was and will be, water, giver, and taker of life in equality of life and death. I am the shroud between this world and the next, and the giver of words from Meredaas to his followers."

"Meredaas, the god of the seas?"

He had heard the name before. Aunt Tua had a book about the gods of the North, and he remembered that image.

"Yes, young Valrin, the great Meredaas, he who, as water, has taken many forms."

"Are you really he?" Valrin asked.

The vibration of the water seemed to change and move quickly. The figure laughed. "I am not, but I do like your questioning. I am a sprite of the temple grounds. None come here. None come from the city named after the Great One. So many are lost."

The figure turned and pointed to Edanos. "I sense it upon him. You bring him to claim the birthrights of all Storm Children?"

"The dwarves threaten the seas. They attack the free peoples; they bring war and bloodshed to the waters. It was by the will of the gods that I found this boy, and he is headstrong and capable. He has a heart about him, and that is needed to bring peace to these waters."

"There will be no peace in these waters, but there will be a change. It was foretold and in time will come to pass. The Storm Children must prepare and be ever watchful of that."

The sprite moved back to the pool before the statue.

"There is a power in the Glacial Seas. These were once high holy lands of the sea peoples of old before they were known as sea people. Their power is still in the lands, but it is hidden. There is magic here untouched by the dread of the old gods of the South. There is purity, but there is also great evil contained throughout these vast frigid waters. The line between the realms of the living and the realms of the gods blur within the depths both above and below the sea.

"Valrin of Travaa, you are young and know not of this world, but beneath your shirt, I sense your offering to the god of the sea, a binding contract to protect the waters of the vast seas, to guard the creatures of the ocean, and to contain an old magic within yourself. You are a Stormborn, one of the very few chosen at the formation of your soul and body to take this charge. Do you wish to embrace the path of the god's servant?"

Valrin wasn't sure, and he looked to Edanos.

"Have you?" he asked him.

"Alas, I could not. It is your choice alone, but know there is much to be done by the one who takes this charge. I cannot force you, but I believe you can, as a fellow Stormborn."

"I will do it," Valrin said.

He finally felt a purpose, finally something beyond eel traps and desolation. He would embrace what he was born to do, though he still did not fully know what that was.

The sprite receded into the pool, and there was a grinding sound behind them. The stairwell they had walked down split in two, revealing a doorway.

Valrin walked forward. Edanos followed behind him. "I have never seen this place in all of the times I have come here."

They went forward, and Valrin pushed open the doorway. There was a glowing room ahead. It was dark but had a blue hue. As they walked into the dome-like structure, a voice spoke from the walls around them.

"Stormborn, you seek the path to your birthright. I tell you this alone. Follow the path north of Merea, through the many teeth of the Jagged Glaciers, and enter the fog realms, following the direction of moonrise. There, look for the whales and fish and the shell horn that sounds at dawn. It is upon that place you will find a doorway with a single star. Present your token and pass through. It is there you find what is yours. Complete your binding, and I take you into my house of protection until it is decreed you are to be no more."

A pedestal rose from the floor, a single crystal.

"This shall be your light in the fog realms. Only place it upon your ship, and the fogs will not hinder your progression."

The room then went dark, and the doors behind them opened.

Valrin took the crystal and turned to see Edanos on one knee.

"That was the voice of the one, the god Meredaas. He gives you this charge."

"I'm not sure where he wants us to go."

"Do not worry, Vals, I will get you there."

"Vals?"

"I can say Valrin if you'd prefer."

"Vals works."

"Come now, boy, let us get to our ship."

They exited the room, and the stairwell closed. They pushed open the doors leading out, and the voice spoke one last time.

"Carry upon the seas with haste and forever embrace that which is the fate of all that live upon the sea."

Edanos shut the doors behind them. "Her riddles and stories, she does love them."

They began back toward the ship when Edanos suddenly diverted from the road and went to an overhanging lookout. He reached into his pocket and pulled out a golden tube that he put to his eye. "Indeed, it seems our friends have followed us this far."

"Are they attacking?" Valrin asked.

"We couldn't be that lucky. They are waiting. We have passage through the cave of the city, but they will be watching. If we keep a good pace, we should be able to shake them. They do have quite a few ships. It seems the secret around your neck has attracted much attention."

Making it back to the docks, Rortho greeted them. "We have hermit crabs on us, Captain. I guess we did not have enough time to fully shake them."

"They do what they do."

Braei approached with a mug of ale.

"I do hope you found more crew where you found the fine drink."

"Aye, Captain, I have at least twenty deckhands, elven lot for the most part and one eager human. He can do tricks with a bow or so the tavern wenches said."

"I don't need tricks nor any one that would have wenches to vouch for his skills," Edanos stated. "I need a good crew."

A man with a long white bow approached them. He had a beard and wore a dark blue coat.

"Captain?" he asked.

"Yes, Edanos of the *Truest Bliss*, and your name is?"

"Fadis, archer, servant to a simple man."

"You're the trickster, then?"

The man smiled and took Braei's ale to his lips, taking a large sip.

"I am, and I've been called worse."

Braei dumped her ale and pushed the man in the chest. "You said you wanted to join our crew, but that does not make you better than a mere deckhand. You can scrub the decks. Work those trickster arms of yours."

Fadis looked at Edanos.

"Well?" Braei asked.

The eager trickster, as he was dubbed by Braei, shrugged and boarded.

"So we make it through the passage and you hope we will get a good lead? Where to afterward?" Rortho asked.

"North, through more treacherous waters."

The dwarf shook his head. "We just got the ship back together. We don't need to tear it apart! But I will rally the crew." The dwarf went up the gangplank. "Prepare to sail!"

Valrin boarded and watched as the crew worked in a rocky harmony as the new crew melded with the old. He went up to the wheel and stood by Edanos.

"The new crew seems to not get along with the old."

"It does happen, but know you must have a good crew who you trust. If you are good to them, they will respect you. We are not pirates like those dwarves. We respect those we work with."

"Yes," Braei mocked, "even if they drink your ale!"

They pulled the holding lines from the moorings and began to move around the actual rocks of the foundation of the city. In the inner portion of the mountain was a large passage that led to the other side. As the ship moved through the passage, Edanos pointed to the ceiling and the carvings in the rocks.

"Vals, it is said that giants carved this passage and set the foundations of the city, but I say giants do not make runes so intricate."

"Who did it, then?"

"I do not know for sure."

"Dwemhar?"

"Ha!" Braei laughed. "Dwemhar? You have the

boy talking about myths."

"No more mythic than the Rusis. I do not know who made these, but within the Glacial Seas, all such things as this are considered work of the sea peoples."

"True you are, about the Rusis," Braei said, "but we actually survived and outlived them. Wouldn't it be a strange thing to come upon one now, after so many years? I do not know of a Rusis that wouldn't obliterate a Dwemhar at first chance."

"Rusis, you talk like dwarves do of elves and as elves do of dwarves in the South. If we are not careful, we shall all be the last of our races. Have you even seen a Rusis other than yourself?"

Braei was silent.

"Take note, then, Vals. Peace. That is what must be aimed for in this world. That is the only way any of us can survive."

"It is a nice gesture for hope," Braei muttered, "but peace only comes for those who win a war."

They came to the end of the passage, and the open sea was before them.

"All sails, tighten ends and keep your cloaks bound!" Rortho shouted. "We move to colder and more violent waters!"

As they pushed forward the sun began to set before them, and they began to make subtle movements around large standing stones that jutted out of the water, not as icy peaks of glaciers or massive mountains, but as literal towers of stone as if a submerged structure with steeples was just below the surface.

There was a storm in the far distance, but it moved away from them. They didn't need the crosswinds to knock them off course, especially now in such turbulent water.

Valrin kept an eye out behind them, as did Edanos. The dwarven ships would likely follow, but they both prayed they would not catch up.

Twice Valrin went to lie down but found himself tossing and turning. He sat up and looked at the amulet. He noticed that the jewel within was pulsing with the beat of his heart. He put his hand against his chest and held the amulet with the other hand, and it was not his imagination. It was the same. He couldn't guess what it meant, but he wondered if the place he was going to would explain it.

He wondered if there would be another sprite, or perhaps Meredaas himself? The book he had read before said the gods could take many forms. He questioned if he would even recognize the god if he was standing before him.

He went back outside and noticed that many of the crew had retired. Edanos was leaning on the back of the ship as Valrin approached him.

"Look, Vals," he said, pointing to the sky. "Do you know of the constellations?"

"I know of some, but this time of the year the first one Aunt Tua told me of is harder to see. I believe she called it Etha's hand? She said it was an elven star pattern praised for its assistance in enchanting."

"Yes, you speak of a power constellation, and when combined with a full moon or a black moon, it increases magical properties by quite a bit. But that is not what is important upon the Glacial Seas. Look upon the horizon, Vals. Just above the crest of the world, you will see a large bright star. That is the sea snail. After that will come the sea horse. Once it is above us, you will have four to six hours until sunrise. Once the polar night begins, there are other ones such as the penguin that would correspond with mid-morning. This becomes more important during that time. The first time I had to deal with the unending night, I about went crazy trying to align myself."

"I understand the path of the stars and the passage of time, but what is a penguin, Edanos?"

"Dear Vals, there is much I must still teach you."

PART 3: SUNRISE

The night was well over them. The sign that Edanos had told him to watch for was now above the ship. He had seen sea horses only once, and now he could make them out in the grouping of stars floating over them.

He had gone to sleep for a while, but Edanos had begun evading more of the towering stone structures, and massive glaciers drew up on either side of them. He couldn't sleep anymore.

Valrin stood by the wheel of the ship.

"Vals, I insist," he said, offering him the wheel. "The best way to learn is sometimes by literally doing it when you have no choice."

"But you're piloting the ship."

Edanos stepped away from the wheel. "No, I'm not."

As the wheel spun and the ship began to move off course, Valrin gripped the wheel and looked forward, keeping the bow of the ship angled between the icy mountains. Though Edanos could grab the wheel at a moment's notice, Valrin wasn't sure he would. He carefully maneuvered the vessel, a harrowing feat considering this was only the second time he was at the helm.

"You're a natural man of the sea. You will be a greater sailor than even I, in time!"

As they maneuvered through the icy chasms, he began to hear a tune. At first, he thought it just the wind, but the longer he listened, he heard more of a song.

Shivering souls upon our sea,
Slicing slashing cut them free
Siren's songs so sweet so soft,
Help their souls to flee aloft.

Bodies aching from lack of touch
Let are hands take care of such!
Come to us and let us play
All of your troubles we shall slay!

"Sirens," Edanos told him nervously.

The glowing hands of the creatures grabbed the railings and smiled, looking up at them.

"The worst part of sirens is that most of your crew will be at severe risk. You are too young for them to affect you, but you are nearing the cusp of manhood. You will deal with them in time. I once fell for the seduction of these sea creatures. They may be of Meredaas, but I still do not care for their sort."

The sirens began to sink away, finding none they were capable of seducing on deck. The glacial path opened up. A great plume of fog hung before them.

"Sea of fogs. I will take the helm. Go place your crystal near the front of the ship. Put it somewhere it will stay put."

Valrin nodded and ran down to the lower deck. A few of the crew had emerged from the lower level, obviously seeking the sirens that were well behind them. He went to the pole for the foremasts and noticed a notch behind one of the ropes that was large enough for the crystal to fit. He placed it and then went back to Edanos.

"Let us see what your gift can do for us. Do you remember the words of Meredaas?"

"'Keep the path of moonrise.' So, we must turn east?"

"Yes, into the fogs we go, and my only prayer is that our path will show!"

As the fogs began to run over the deck, the crystal glowed and a bright fiery light pierced the fog in a large open swathe, clearing the sea and opening a path for the ship. Almost immediately, Edanos wheeled left to avoid a large rock jutting up from the sea. Valrin looked behind them and noticed the veil of the fogs covering their path.

"No ship in their right mind would enter this region without some form of a device such as this."

"So I assume we will have no more pursuers?"

"Never assume, especially when dealing with the one known as Rugag. Always keep the sails ready. That pirate has chased after us for some time, and I can say he is anything but dumb. Here, Vals, take the helm again. I will get us some coffee."

Valrin stood at the helm, looking through the vast bleakness before him, and was amazed at the magic of the crystal and its ability to burn away the fog.

He had gone from a boy gathering eels to sailing with one of the greatest captains he could ever imagine in the span of just a few days. He did think back to his aunt, Tua, though. He was saddened by her death, but he tried to believe as Edanos did. There were reasons for the workings, but he felt they were beyond his understanding.

Edanos brought both of them mugs. The hot coffee was a welcome drink in the frigid cold he felt to his very core.

"A bit of cinnamon in this cup. A rarer herb from the very far south. It will help stave off a sore throat, or so they say."

The taste was strange but good. As he piloted the ship through an almost constant path of fog, they began to pass through a series of large archways. The remnants of other vessels dotted the rocks. Weathered and long-rotting wood with the frayed ice-covered ropes were an ominous sign.

"This region of fog has only existed for the past forty or fifty years. I remember a time when ships just called this a cursed region. It didn't keep ships from sailing here. Treasure hunters, mainly. The fogs came upon the surface, and afterward I can say far fewer dared to come here."

"Where did the fogs come from?"

"If I knew where these fogs came from, I would tell you. It is one of many mysteries of these seas. Perhaps one day you will discover it!"

"I could never do what you do. I can barely guide the ship! I'm not even too sure I could get us back out from where we've come so far."

Edanos smiled at him. "Time is both your enemy and friend. It takes time to learn how to navigate the many oceans, but it also wears on your men. It takes time to develop a cunning for how to deal with the many dangers of sailing, particularly where dwarves are concerned, but I'd say I have done it well. But that has taken time from what some may call a more normal life. Marriage. Children."

"Do you find yourself wanting that?"

"Sometimes."

There was a silence between them. Valrin watched as wisps of fog rolled between them. There was a flash of lightning behind them, and Edanos looked down at him.

"I then remember that I am not of this world. I am Stormborn. I am a man of the sea. In my travels of late, I have sunk a ship of the Barb king and rescued another like me." He nodded toward him. "I am happy with the events so far. I have dreamed for many nights of going where we go. In the end, I hope it is worth it."

They had been progressing through the fogs at a rapid rate. They were to progress until dawn and then look and listen for signs of a horn sounding and whales within the waters. The dawn sun was still some time off, but there was a glow in the sky.

"I do not know what this is, but the lord of the sea did not tell us of any such sight as this," Edanos told him.

The *Truest Bliss* began to grind the sea bottom, and Edanos turned the wheel to the right, attempting to navigate the obstruction. The bow seemed to grind and churn, the current of the ocean pushing them back and forth and forcing the aft of the ship to slap up against a rock.

The crew rushed to the deck and grabbed large spears. They went to the side of the ship and drove the spear points into the rocky ice. The currents shifted around them, and for the moment, they could not move away from the rocks.

Valrin looked through a split in the rocks and noticed a glowing crystal.

Braei wiped the sleep from her eyes and then looked at Edanos as she pointed. "A strange path, Captain. Did you mean for us to come here."

"No," he said, walking to where he could get a better view.

Rortho climbed up on the pathway, nervously

looking down to see what he could spot from afar.

Fadis strung his bow and jumped onto the path.

"Only the captain can order crew to leave the ship when we are at sea," Braei told him.

"The captain needs eyes that can see beyond the fog, and weapons that can reach enemies that are just out of reach. I can do both for our captain."

Valrin looked down the path, and Edanos looked to Rortho.

"You have the helm. Keep the ship steady. Once the current shifts, keep yourselves against the rocks and light torches along the bow. We did not end up here by accident. I will take them and check whatever this place is."

"Aye, Captain. Just don't go joining the fish. It'd be a shame in this desolate cold place."

Fadis walked ahead of them, moving up the path until he came to a large stone. He ran up to the top of it and knelt down. As Edanos and Valrin nearly got to the spot where he was, he turned and jumped down. "It looks good; there is no one here."

Braei shook her head. "I wouldn't expect someone here. It is a bit desolate."

"I'm just trying to keep myself as a worthy member of the group. Besides, my eyes can see the no snow or ice has been disturbed along path in some time. If you do not want further help from me—"

"We're just a few yards from the ship, so it is likely that no one would be immediately attack us until we were further in, but thank you," Edanos said.

Braei shook her head.

There were many more glowing stones the further they went along the path. The road itself had dropped in to actually run slightly below the edges of a wall that came up to Valrin's chest. The road climbed up and through several swathes of ocean, breaking stone pillars.

In the distance, there were several dark statues just visible in the moonlight. The road passed between two of them, and further on, a large domed structure was encrusted with a deep layer of ice.

A frigid wind gusted over them. Valrin brought his coat around him and kept his head down, but he tried to follow Edanos the best he could.

Fadis made a loud sound with an audible shiver. "So cold! Hey, Braei, do you think we could share some heat together? I could use some warmth."

"Bastard human," she responded. "Keep your thoughts to yourself or I will give you some heat."

"Hmm, sounds like an invite for a bit more fun."

Edanos stopped and turned. He drew his blade and pointed it at Fadis.

"Once more remark, and I will dispose of you into these waters. You test my patience beyond what any of the rest of the crew has."

Fadis had his hands up. "No worries, good sir. I'm just testing what I can do with your lady."

"She isn't mine."

Edanos began to walk again, and Braei pointed for Valrin to follow him.

"Boy," Fadis said to him.

"Yes?"

"Learn well from the captain. He has a moral resolve that is admirable. Not claiming himself a woman and all. I'm just a bastard. I struggle the line of what is right and what is. . . what is not so great. I have tried for a few years to right my wrongs but it seems I have failed in that so far. I do care though. I hope you've learned that from the recent interchanges between us all."

Valrin ignored him. He thought about responding, but that would've just opened up another avenue of conversation, and his mind wasn't on actual talking.

He looked up at the massive statues and noticed they each wore crowns with large spikes that came off their heads. Snow drifts twisted around their bodies, and the road was covered with ice here. He could hear the pounding of the waves beneath them. The salty spray reached up to the path.

Braei used her powers to melt the ice and give them a wet but walkable path. They came to the large door. There were two torch basins, but neither of them were lit. Not surprising considering where they were. Edanos took out a torch stick, and Braei lit it for him. The bright fire felt good against Valrin's face. They were about to enter. Valrin felt a tug in his stomach, wondering what was beyond the closed doors. He questioned if it would be a treasure of some kind, but in truth, he just hoped for something of interest and not deadly. To find an abandoned structure this far out in the middle of the Glacial Seas was strange to all of them.

"It is not elven," Edanos said. "I cannot even read this text."

"It is of the sea people," Fadis said. "There is writing like this back in the floating city. Some say it is Dwemhar, but I've always known it as sea speech."

Edanos pushed open the door. It was a simple enough feat, but it was just the first of a set of doors. As they went to the second door, the first one simply flapped in the wind. The second door was a bit more difficult, but it, too, was forced open by Edanos and Fadis.

As the archer stepped into the next room, he immediately notched an arrow and snaked his way to the right of the door. Edanos pointed his sword in front of him. He scanned the surroundings, and then Braei and Valrin followed.

There were old bodies everywhere. Most of the bones were no more than dust, but a few still had shape. They did wear a silverish armor, but there were no markings on them.

"What do you think killed them, Captain?" Braei asked.

Edanos knelt at one of them, feeling along the bones. "I do not know. These skeletons are so old,

I cannot even guess.

Valrin walked away from them and thumbed through a book on the table. *Enchanting*, the book was titled. He glanced up at a large basin in the center of the room. He then saw a crystal underneath its edge and went to it. As he rubbed his finger on the edge of it, the crystal started glowing before a roaring fire came to life in the basin.

"Wow," Edanos said, "a strange find, indeed!"

The warmth from the fire was nice, and Valrin was so close that the last thing he wanted was to move away from it. But Fadis had noticed something, and so had Braei. A doorway, that, unlike the other wooden doors, was not very dark, had appeared surrounded by torches. As Edanos approached it, the doorway opened, resulting in a lighted hallway with large glowing stones above their heads.

"The strangest thing," Fadis said.

Several tall figures appeared before them, and at first, there was a general shuffling of weapons, but the specters did not seem to see them or care to interact with them. They began to walk down the passage.

"Should we follow?" Braei asked.

Edanos led them. It was a long passage overall, with no windows or drawings or anything to distract them from simply following their guides. There was another room here. This one had large, ice-sheeted windows on the far half edge of the room. The ocean was visible here, with a ribbon of green polar lights visible just above it.

"What is this place?" asked Braei.

Edanos shook his head. Valrin looked to those around him, but it seemed they were as perplexed as he was.

"I will have order in this assembly!" a voice rang out.

It was sudden, and the speaker materialized before them, but he was speaking away from them. The specters they had seen before began to appear clearer than they had seen them.

It was a large group of people. They were not elves or dwarves. They appeared as men but wore strange tall headdresses that were weird geometrical shapes. Everything about them was alien to him.

"We must flee this place. The wars have come to close! The waters will flood the cities on lower ground," one of them said.

"You think as the elves. We are above them, and we must act it," another said.

The original speaker who had called them to order stretched out his hands.

"It is written that we shall uphold ourselves with mindfulness when faced with tragedy. One cannot descend to panic, to simple pleasures of the flesh. We cannot lose faith in what energy we put toward our minds."

"But, master, the storms are getting closer. We cannot pray to the gods; they have abandoned us.

We are here alone."

"We are not alone, for we will always be a part of this place. Our spirits will live on, and our presence will become as the sea. Forever. Our ancestors are within every rock of the mountains high. The world is but a step from us. The realm of the gods is within reach to us if only we claim it."

The original man who had called for them to flee now spoke again. "We are without the ability to claim such a thing. We are without connection to our brethren. We will die here and become part of the sea. With storms we shall be remembered, thunder rolling across vast oceans. I have seen it. I have seen the future. Our world will fade away, and few of any who call themselves of our blood will ever know we existed."

Lightning flashed outside the windows, and Valrin wasn't sure if it was real or if it was part of whatever vision they were witnessing.

"So be the end of this place. The sea that will be, will be home to our guidance, and we will lock away our knowledge until the time is meant for it to be restored. We will no longer ascend as have others. I say to you each, go upon the world at death and become part of it, waiting to give our knowledge to the ones marked by the storms. The gods work in ways beyond us, but we have all dreamed of storms and children. It is a sign of what is to come."

The group nodded to what their master said.

"In time we will have a purpose. When this path is walked again, it will be that time. We shall help those who cannot help themselves. We will do the will of the gods, but I fear it will be a time of great sorrow for those whose path we guide. For our path is never one of ease. May the faith of the Dwemhar always guide."

The vision ceased, and the room became dark again.

"What in the gods was that?" Fadis asked.

"I don't know," Edanos said. He stared at Valrin. "Vals, do you feel that they spoke of the Stormborn, of you and I?"

"They spoke of children and storms."

"We are on the right path, then," he said. "Let us return to our ship. We were meant to see this, but I feel we must get moving on our quest. We are near the end to what I have sought for my entire life. Vals, let us get to where we need to go."

"Dwemhar, strange," Braei said. "Maybe they aren't the myth I thought."

They exited the room, and Valrin felt something he had never felt before. He had more purpose than even standing before the sprite of Meredaas in Merea. He did not know much of this Dwemhar term or even what he had seen. He wasn't even sure of the name itself.

As they exited the structure, passing between the two statues, he asked Edanos of them. "Were they the sea people we hear of in rumor?"

"Vals, in all my days, I have never seen

something like those. I would guess they were the sea people, and I feel we may see something like that again, in time. We must keep the path."

"Keep the path?" Fadis said. "Are you a priest?"

"No, Fadis, but you could use a path yourself. It seems you were a bit too zealous to join on a random adventure leading to death."

"Fair enough, I guess. I had myself a good time at the brothel in town. Death is okay for now. You should teach your son there about that."

Edanos grabbed him by the shoulder and spun him around. "You would mind your tongue. There are some in the world not tainted by your thinking. You are foul and unworthy. If we all survive this, I will be sure to give you pay and send you on your way once we make port. I do not care for you."

Edanos walked past him, beckoning Valrin to follow him.

Fadis shook his head as Braei walked past him.

"You did not tell him you're not my father?" Valrin asked.

"No, I care little to speak to him more than I need to. Let him assume."

They were nearly halfway across the walkway, and their ship was clearly ahead. Valrin was freezing. The expanse of the open ocean was frigid, and there was no warmth left in his body.

"No," Edanos said slowly.

Valrin looked up at him and noticed he was staring to the west. "What is it?"

Edanos didn't answer. "Let us move, quickly,"

he shouted.

The group made it to the ship in very quick time. Rortho bowed to Edanos.

"Captain, we have a good tide. We're ready to cast off."

Edanos was at the helm. "Then cast off now!"

"You heard the captain, raise the sails, get them up, quickly, quickly," Rortho ordered.

Fadis went to help the crew as Braei and Valrin joined Edanos at the helm.

"What is it?" Valrin asked.

"Dwarves. Behind us. Coming quickly."

Braei and Valrin looked behind them, seeing flames just visible in the veil of the fogs.

"How could they navigate and find us? How could they know where we were?"

"I have a guess," Edanos said. "There are such things that one can place and then follow through the works of magic. Not all aboard are crew who can be trusted, but it is too late to turn back now."

Valrin could tell they were talking about Fadis. He looked at the archer as he secured the sails. He wasn't sure what to make of him.

They pulled away from the ruins and came to an open expanse of ocean. The dwarven ships were drawing closer but still far behind them for the moment. There was a flat sea here. The twilight rim of an approaching dawn lit the sky in a purple hue, and at that moment, the water around them began to undulate and break.

Valrin went to the rail of the ship and looked

over. Large creatures swam beside them.

"Whales," Braei told him. "Hundreds of them, maybe more. Edanos, look!"

But Edanos was looking behind him. The dwarven ship was not alone and the many vessels pursuing them were not slowing.

"I cannot believe they are moving at such a pace. It is unnatural."

"It is in unnatural waters we find ourselves, Captain," Rortho said.

The whales at either side of them were of every size and species. The water began to sparkle with a strange hue that led to a massive tower that appeared in the growing dawn sky.

"That wasn't there before," Rortho said.

"It was not." Edanos nodded. "Tighten sails, make sure we have no more wind escaping than needed. We must get to the shoreline without fail."

Valrin went back to the helm with Edanos. He turned to see their pursuers and turned back to see Edanos looking at him.

"Do not worry about them. If what I believe is right, you will be safe, but I must get you there."

"We will get there, and we can discover whatever it is that is so guarded by Meredaas."

"Perhaps, but I may not be able to immediately follow. Nothing is certain for us."

A horn sounded. Not a dwarven horn nor an elven horn. In fact, it was no horn that any aboard had ever heard. It started deep, rumbling the ocean surface itself, and then, like a shift in the wind, it sounded again only with a higher pitch.

A sound came from beneath the ocean, and the water bubbled around them as large crags began to emerge, piercing through the surface of the clear expanse, turning it into what looked like several mountain ranges.

Edanos spun the wheel of the ship in an effort to move the ship from running aground.

"Hold your lines. We are in for rough sailing!" Rortho shouted out.

Edanos moved the wheel of the ship the opposite way as it seemed they now followed a strange road in the ocean made up of the stone fences of sudden obstacles.

The island drew closer, and as they snaked through the strange pathway in the ocean, a deep fog rolled over them.

"Valrin! See to the crystal!"

Valrin ran to the front of the ship and checked the crystal. Passing his hand over it, the crystal spun to life, casting a bright flame toward the fogs. They receded, though much lower than before.

The rocky sailing passage began to recede as they came to the end of a line of jagged points.

"A bit of insurance?" asked Braei. "To assure those not worthy do not make it here?"

"I suppose," Edanos said to her. "We draw close to this place we have sought. Hopefully, the dwarves will not reach these waters."

The shoreline was ahead. A large pillar with a massive shell rose out of the water. The wind gusted, and the shell began to make a deep horn sound. They had made it.

As Valrin stood at the fore of the ship, Fadis came to his side.

"You believe in this strange journey to who knows, don't you?"

"I have no reason not to."

Fadis smirked. "I'd say that's true, but is it worth what we do? Heading to the far northern seas to nearly get killed for no reason in a rickety ship?"

"I'd say that you offered to come, and I'd argue that this was a, as you said, rickety ship."

"I was paid to come," he corrected, "but you are unlike me. You have some choice, do you not?"

"I do not."

"You were taken against your will?"

"No, but I have no one else and nothing else to do."

"A man always has a choice. It is simply if he has the courage to make it. I think you do, Valrin."

"A profound statement," Braei said from behind them.

"It is," Fadis said. "I will get back to cleaning the deck. I assume we will have a bit more ice building up, and it isn't going to scrape itself."

"Yes, it is good you find something of use to do."

As Fadis went back to ship duties, Braei stood with Valrin. The shoreline was ahead. It was bleak, with white sand and tall cliffs that reached up into the clouds. There was only one beach and two large white pillars off to one side of the beach.

As the ship drew close to shallows, Edanos ordered the sails lowered and passed the wheel to Rortho.

"I do not see our pursuers, but I expect them in time."

"We won't let them get close, Captain. I'll keep them from the shore."

Fadis strung his bow as the others prepared a small boat to row to shore.

"No," said Edanos.

"No?" the man asked. "Did I cause any trouble before?"

"Of course not, but I need you here. If the dwarves get close, you will be a useful asset."

Fadis was surprised and scanned the horizon. "No dwarves yet. I could just return and—"

"You will follow my orders. Rortho has command until I return."

Valrin got into the boat with Braei and several of the crew. Edanos joined them, and they were lowered into the water.

With a splash sending icy spray over Valrin's already windblown face, he looked around at the strange surroundings. Glowing plants grew up the side of the cliff face, and it seemed that though the presence of life was strangely strong here, he could see no other living animals. The whales from before had split off before the sudden eruption of rocks from the ocean floor.

As they drew close to the shore, a rogue current

pushed them further to the shoreline, and in an instant, their small boat was left on the sands of the island's beach.

Valrin looked up the cliffs, immediately seeing what Meredaas had told him he would. A lone door marked with a star. As he and Valrin stepped out, the others of the crew drew their weapons.

"I see no reasons for enemies here," Edanos cautioned, "but be mindful. This place is more unknown to my sense than the entirety of the ocean depths."

The door itself was up a small dune of sand and flatly placed into the cliffs. Valrin approached it with Braei at his side, and the door simply cracked open. He looked down at his amulet and noticed it was bright blue now.

As they entered into a dark chamber, the door shut behind them to the sudden dismay of the crew. There were only ten others, but many of them were the new crew picked up at Merea before.

"Do not fear," Edanos told them. "If I am right and all I have studied is right, we are safe here."

The walls were splashed with torchlight that seemed to come to life with their presence in the long hall that reached out from them.

"Sea people?" asked Braei.

He nodded to her. "Perhaps, but I doubt any of them still exist. The vision at the tower before confirmed that; at least, I believe it did. We will find something else. Something we have searched for. Something I have searched for."

They progressed down the long hall. The light of the torches was nothing like the light coming from Valrin's amulet. He lifted it up, holding it as an additional light source until they came to another door. This one had the image of a large fish upon it. He pushed it open and felt a rush of warm, salty wind. They were in another chamber. A larger room of sorts, with a massive fire burning from a cylindrical pit that had no obvious fuel source. There were steps to their right, and after several paths that took them further and further down, they came to another gateway. This was bound by golden bars.

Valrin could hear the water on the other side. As he touched the bars, nothing happened.

"Your amulet, try it," Edanos said.

He took his amulet and did as Edanos said, placing it against the bars. They began to glow and then slowly receded into the gateway.

He stepped in with Edanos at his heel. They were met by something neither of them expected. Braei immediately lifted her hands to summon spells, and the crew with them cowered.

PART 4: VALRIN OF THE SEAS

Valrin gasped as Edanos fell to his knees.

Before them was that which could only be described as a massive fish. Its head sat on the surface of the water, and on his head was a large crown of gold. Appearing suddenly, as if a veil was lifted, was elaborate stonework decorating the entire cave, reaching up above them and around the entire room.

"Meredaas of the many oceans. We are not worthy!"

The god of the sea was before them. The god many had spoken of in Valrin's life. Normally in curse or prayer but never as an actual sight to actually see in breathing form just as the whales from before.

"My eternal home quakes," Meredaas said. "Come, Valrin and Edanos, Stormborn, come to my depths."

The god-fish sank into the water as two figures emerged from the surface. They were like the sirens from before but much more beautiful. The females were nude except for long hair hanging down from their heads, just covering them.

As Valrin stepped forward, one of them handed him a large shell.

"Keep this upon your chest," she told him. "It will allow you to enter our grace's presence."

Valrin placed the shell on his chest, and suddenly it was difficult for him to breathe. He removed the shell.

"I can't breathe."

Edanos did as Valrin had and then jumped into the water.

"Your friend does not bear the amulet, but he has the idea that you must embrace. With the shell, you are not of the land but of the sea. Join the depths. You will find the water warm within this place."

Valrin placed the shell on his chest again and jumped in. At once, he felt himself floating downward, further down than ever possible without the shell. He took a deep breath, and he was able to breathe though he felt a strange tinge as he did. The shell suctioned to his chest, and he was able to put his hands out. He flapped his arms as he went, feeling the water float through his fingertips as Edanos looked up from below him and smiled.

Schools of fish floated between them. Sharks,

octopuses, and even several more mermaids swam around them.

Valrin looked down further and could see glowing shells and hundreds of merpeople. He then looked into an area of coral along the bottom of the depths and saw the massive sea god, Meredaas, floating on the sea floor.

As his feet came to rest on the soft sand, he walked with Valrin to a large platform of archways and spinning spheres of coral. A white fire shot up and around them.

"You have unlocked the way to the future, dear Valrin and Edanos of the *Truest Bliss*. Captain of the surface realm, you have aided the young one along this path. You have the thanks of all for your efforts. You sacrifice much to complete this task."

"For the glory of the sea and your reign, Meredaas."

"My reign means little to those upon the oceans now, but I thank you. You are both of what you saw within the old tower of the sea peoples. How foolish were they to use my graceful and terrible ocean for their own destructive needs? Much like others who seek to plunder my home for their own advantage. It is souls like them who will derail that which has been set about in the world of the gods. I have found hope in you who come for that which was promised and foretold. You will have something that none else have. A tool, a treasure to some, but of something that requires the very life of one of you."

"We must die?" Valrin asked.

He didn't mean to sound so shocked or to speak so suddenly, but instead of some form of retribution or cruel words, the fish seemed to laugh, if it could be called laughter.

"No, my young one, but it will require something of a promise, a binding to your life. Remove your amulet so it may serve its true purpose for your life."

Valrin removed the amulet, and it floated away from him, resting in front of Meredaas.

"Those of the sea from before were wise to work to restore my faith in their race. So close they were to me in the beginning, it is horrid that they are all gone from the world; at least, as they are now. There will come a time when others are prepared, but not yet."

The amulet floated down and into the sand. There was a shock that Valrin felt in his feet, and then the sand began to rumble. The surface of the underwater expanse began to shift, and in a large plume of bubbling sand, something emerged and rose to the surface.

Meredaas spoke. "In time there will be much need of a captain of the seas. You are young, but you have the soul that is strong enough to do what you must in the coming years. Edanos of the *Truest Bliss*, long have you sought my seas for the chance to do what another will do instead. But I will bless you in time. You must protect this young one and his gift. You are not done in your life's quest. All will be known in time."

Valrin felt himself rising up, coming to the surface of the water. Hands came under him and Edanos. Mermaids propelled them up and out of the water. The shells that had helped them breathe fell off, and Valrin's eyes became huge as he looked down at the glowing golden object that the mermaids drop him toward. He was nearly to whatever it was, and the mermaid released him. He floated down gracefully, standing on the strange glowing structure. As he stood there, the glowing subsided, and he noticed he was on a ship.

Edanos looked around and dropped to the deck of it. "So long I have awaited the chance to be on the deck of such a vessel as this. This is one of the Realm Vessels of the sea peoples. I had only read about them, but they have powers beyond any simple ship."

Valrin was not sure what to think. The vessel seemed like it had not sailed at all. The deck was of the purest wood and had not a single scratch. The sails were strange and did not have all the extra pulleys and ropes as did the *Truest Bliss*, and did not have weapons. He walked to one of the posts and saw his amulet in the wood. He reached out to take it when Meredaas bumped the side of the ship.

"Valrin of Travaa, you have made the journey of the Stormborn. You stand now on the vessel of your ancestors, a jewel of the sea, enchanted with the powers of old to uphold the sanctity of my oceans. You are of the sea. You are the sword of the sea. Your connection is like no other for you. If you choose to become the captain of the vessel, you will be connected to the ship. You will not need sleep as you do in your human form. You will be a stalwart beacon tied to my realm in living and in death. If you accept such a task, know only that you may never recant your vow. As Stormborn, you will accept your title and your fate in that time where you must give your life for those who will go forward."

There was a sudden deep silence unlike any Valrin had ever heard. He closed his eyes. He had spent so many days simply living on the island back home. He always listened to the stories of the sea, the captains, the bards, the drunken men spouting off about what they had seen. Aunt Tua was always there, protecting him, and in her final act of protection, she had given her life.

He looked to Edanos, and he saw tears running down his face.

"Vals, do not fret over me. Just to be within the presence of our mutual god is overwhelming for me. I wished, oh, how I wished to be in your boots and to take this on, but know I will be with you on your journey. I will protect you if you take this oath. You can do it, Vals."

Valrin took hold of the amulet. He wanted to simply pull it from its resting place in the ship. His heartbeat was in sync with the amulet. He was giving a part of himself for a calling that only a few days ago he knew nothing of. He closed his eyes and could feel the water against the bow of the boat. Further out, he could feel the oceans of the Glacial Seas and the ice moving in the great depths. He heard the songs of the whales as they spoke to one another and the scratching of the large octopuses moving along the deepest ravines beyond the reach of light.

He pushed the amulet into the wood of the ship and removed his hand.

"I, Valrin of Travaa, Stormborn, accept this ship and the charge of Meredaas to protect his seas and to command this ship of old."

There was a flash of light, and the surroundings so glorious and dazzling faded away.

"Trust in me, Valrin," Meredaas said.

The ship moved against the shoreline. It rested against the stone docks as Braei and the others ran down toward them. The splendor they had seen before had vanished to the cave and only the golden gates.

"The ship! Edanos, the ship you always spoke of! The one you talked of from the old stories!"

Edanos wiped his eyes. "I have walked a righteous path in honor of the sea, and I know this path was what we should follow."

From the opposite side of the large cave system came the sounds of scratching stone. The rocky cave wall slid down, letting in a blistering wind from the outside seas. The torches around them went dark, and they once again were exposed to the frigid cold of the Glacial Seas.

Valrin went to the helm of the ship, and the sails seemed to react to just his touch on the wheel.

"Come aboard," Edanos told everyone. Braei jumped on, rubbing her fingers across the railings. The ship was no longer gold but instead was a deep red oak. There were several crystals at the helm, but Valrin had no idea what they did. As the crew joined them, it was strange for them to have no immediate need to do anything to help the ship go underway.

"Take us out, Valrin. We will meet up with the *Truest Bliss* and decide what we must do next. The dwarves will no doubt be close. We must hope that we do not need to fight, but if we do, I will help you."

As he gave thought to the direction of the ship, it seemed to respond slightly with drifting that way but then more so as he actually turned the wheel. He had the strangest feelings as they began to depart.

He maneuvered the ship as it sliced through the water to the cave opening. It was agile, slender, and moved with such ease, there was no comparing it to even the *Truest Bliss*. As they went through the opening in the cave, they began out a long rocky crevice with only the sky above them. Valrin looked ahead at open sea and to clear waters. He would need to turn left as they exited, at best he could figure. As Edanos came to his side, he felt confident. He did not know what was to happen in the coming days, but he felt hope.

It was then several thuds struck the ship from above. Valrin looked up to see dwarves swinging down from rocks above. Braei shot several fiery spells at the intruders as the crew brandished their weapons.

Edanos drew his blade and pointed. "Get us to the *Truest Bliss*!"

Valrin gripped the wheel, keeping the ship moving forward but watching as more dwarves poured from above. Their crew fell to the deck, splashing blood as more dwarves swarmed the deck. One of them spotted Valrin and ran up the stairwell to him. Edanos parried his swinging ax, deflecting it away before slashing the man in the neck.

The ship made its way from its rocky birth to the open sea. But the sea was not as open as he had thought. Eight black dwarven vessels were in a half circle, sealing the harbor. The *Truest Bliss* had been boarded.

Valrin heard a click, and a crossbow bolt struck Edanos in the shoulder. The captain of the *Truest Bliss* fell to the deck of Valrin's ship.

A dwarf began to laugh. There was another ship approaching. It was a large ship. It was the ship that before had been in the harbor at Travaa.

"Well, well, well, it seems the ole' dwarf captain had his suspicions, and they turned out just as he suspected," the dwarf shouted from afar.

Several clawed chains were thrown into the deck but could not grasp the wood. They simply slid and fell off the side.

"So it is nigh uncatchable!" The dwarf laughed. "But it is the ship."

"Stop the hollering, Rugag. It is me you want," Edanos shouted.

"Oh, Edanos, it was you once, but it is the wee lad now. He has my ship, the ship my king deserves. The ship that my king's desire for resulted in some of your own poor crew being left on a deserted island just to be picked up, for the righteous Edanos couldn't leave poor saps just to die."

The ship had slowly drifted toward the *Truest Bliss*, and the ship of Rugag had gone with it. The current was very strong, so Valrin assumed it was actually partially his thought that moved the ship.

As they drew closer, Valrin and Braei, who was being held at spear point, noticed the dwarves on the ship holding the crew hostage were the same ones that Edanos had saved.

Rortho looked out, and Fadis was at his side.

"They betrayed us, Edanos!" Rortho shouted. "The bastards gave us up. They had some type of dwarven device in their jewelry. We've been sold out by your kindness."

"You cannot take the boy," Edanos said. "He isn't yours; he isn't mine. He is his own. He is of the great god Meredaas."

The dwarf laughed again with a boisterous tone. "Meredaas, the giant fish? I no longer believe in the fallacies of the weak. If the one of the seas wants to do something about me, let the bastard squid lover!"

Edanos crawled to Valrin. "You must live, no matter what. You must escape this place with the ship. The fate of the Stormborn, the fate of our futures, rest with you, Valrin."

One of the dwarves who was nearest walked over to Edanos and kicked him.

"Shut up, you damn fool! No more rattlin'!" The dwarf then went toward Valrin.

"Take the boy, and then we will take the ship. We will kill the rest and feed them to the sharks, and then when the sharks are done, we'll take the sharks. Can't have good trading supplies go to waste!"

The dwarf stomped toward him. Valrin grimaced. Drawing his sword, he held it out toward his foe.

"Now, little boy, we don't want you to hurt yourself. Give me the blade, and it will be enough. You don't want to kill, and we do not want you to."

He held the blade up, but he was shaking. He knew very little, save a few sword fights back at home that were all for play. There was that one swordsman—it was an elf. He knew a lot and said his sons were like Valrin's age in appearance and already as proficient as any man. It was hard for Valrin to believe that. He turned his thought to his adversary. He was breathing heavily, and he made steps back as the dwarf approached. He closed his eyes.

Meredaas, help.

The ship shook and rocked beneath his feet. The dwarf lost balance and fell. The other dwarves still hanging on from above struggled to hold on as the ship began to toss in the water. There was a blast of water to their right, and several of the whales from before struck Rugag's ship. Meredaas has heard him.

Braei took the moment to cast a stormy barrage of lightning into different dwarves on the ship. The dwarf who had stumbled now grabbed his foot. Valrin stabbed him with the point of his blade, severing the dwarf's fingers. He then slashed it across the back of the exposed hairy neck, sending a splatter of blood on either side of the man.

He ran to Edanos, helping his friend up. The bolt was in his chest, and Edanos struggled to breathe.

Rugag had been distracted by the onslaught of sea creatures attacking his boat. Several large octopuses climbed up the side, and the whales kept his ship from being steadied.

Over on the *Truest Bliss*, the few remaining loyal crew fought to take back the ship. The outer line of dwarven ships began to fire their bolts, sending massive chained hooks hurling through the air.

Rortho shouted over, "Get to our ship. We are clear of breathing dwarves, 'cept myself."

Fadis jumped to the ship with Valrin and ran

toward where Edanos was. As he came up, he drew his bow, aiming toward Valrin. Valrin dropped as the bolt passed just to his side, taking down the dwarf who had tried to capture him.

"If you're going to have a sword, best actually use it to kill the dwarves," Fadis told him.

Fadis and Braei took hold of Edanos. "Get me to my ship and then stay with Valrin. He needs your help. He is your captain."

Braei shook her head. "Get Edanos to the *Truest Bliss*! We will need both ships to break through the dwarven fleet! You're not dying, Edanos! We will all get out of this!"

Valrin followed behind them as they went to the front of the vessel. Rortho was waiting, and though the ships bounced precariously close to one another, they did not strike, and they were able to move Edanos to his ship. A bolt flew into the side of the *Truest Bliss*, sending wood splintering into the air.

"Follow us!" Rortho shouted.

Edanos was struggling to stand aboard his ship, but was staring at Valrin. "Follow me out, Vals. I will show you the way."

"And I will show you how to send their ships to the bottom of the sea!" Rortho shouted.

The dwarf, first mate of the damaged vessel *Truest Bliss*, ran to man the crossbows. Most of the crew remained aboard the ship, but none had the zeal of the dwarf.

Fadis drew his bow, firing at several dwarves

already aiming at them. Valrin watched as he drew arrow after arrow, releasing in quick succession. He then ran to the railings and fired a set of two arrows, striking more dwarves aboard the enemy vessel. "Come, Valrin. You must get to the helm!"

He ran to the wheel. Taking it in hand, he turned away from the *Truest Bliss*, running his ship against the vessel of Rugag.

"Bastard boy!" he heard the dwarf shouting.

The *Truest Bliss* pulled in front of them. Edanos was at the helm, and Rortho ran along the crossbows, sending bolts into the vessels that were approaching them. It took great strength for the dwarf, firing the massive bolts and then pulling back on the twined chains by himself. Many of the crew were falling to arrow fire from the dwarven vessels. There wasn't any more of the crew on Valrin's vessel. None except Fadis and Braei, at least.

Edanos made an obvious pointing motion that Valrin followed. His ship moved quickly, almost overtaking whom he was following, and the dwarves were closing in.

It was a narrow passage that they were sailing toward, a spot where there was only one dwarven vessel and then open sea. It wasn't an opening before, but when the ocean creatures began attacking, the other ships had moved to help Rugag.

"Fire!" he heard from behind him. He turned to see several streaks of fiery arrows fly over his ship and strike the *Truest Bliss*. It was a moment later when another wave came, this one sending a bolt over Valrin's head. Braei went to the side of the ship and cast a blast of fire into the ocean, creating a large veil of steam rising up into the air. It did a good job of shrouding their vessels.

Edanos was moving the ship to the left again, taking a path around the towering island. If they could get distance between them and the other ships, they had a chance.

Another line of bolts came flying toward them, but due to the Rusis' distraction, their bolts missed.

Valrin felt confident. He felt relaxed to some point. They had somehow escaped the clutches of Rugag, and through no real understanding himself, Meredaas had answered his short and sudden prayer.

A horn called. This one he had heard before. Braei jerked her glance toward the *Truest Bliss*. Several more dwarven ships appeared in a line, running a passage to block them in. These had been hidden. Waiting. It was like it was all part of Rugag's game.

Valrin looked behind and saw the rest of the dwarven fleet bringing in the net of ships. There was a narrow opening to open ocean, but there was a dwarven vessel running parallel to them, attempting to cut them off.

The *Truest Bliss* changed course. Its sails were at full. It ran a path almost directly with Valrin, but Rortho was no longer at the crossbows. His ax was out, and he stood at the front of the ship. He was holding the ropes and bracing himself.

As Valrin kept his course, aiming for the ever-closing opening, Edanos rammed the *Truest Bliss* into the dwarven vessel. Edanos then drew his blade and ran with Rortho, jumping onto the dwarven vessel that they had thrown off course, leaving the way open for Valrin. He moved his ship around the floating wreckage and to open sea. As he twisted the wheel back to the left, he noticed Edanos and Rortho fighting multiple dwarves.

Fadis fired several arrows, striking dwarves all along the opposite deck.

Valrin had taken the wrong path. He now ran along the line of dwarven vessels instead of out and further away. A barrage of bolts came screaming over the top of the deck, just nearly missing the masts and the small crew Valrin had to start with.

Braei was on the railing. She appeared extremely weak, but she was still casting spells. The Rusis' strength was failing her. Fadis held strong.

"We need to get out of here, Captain," Fadis said.

He was the captain. The captain of the Stormborn vessel. But he had a choice, and though he didn't know what he was doing, he had to try. He wheeled the ship into the dwarven line.

"Valrin! That is not what I had in mind!" Fadis shouted.

He did not know what would happen, but he

looked to the crystals at the helm. Twisting the first one, the masts began to shine brightly, and a blast of fire shot out of the side of the ship. A moment later, the hull of the ship struck the dwarven vessel. The ships tore at one another, leaving chunks of the dwarven vessel in the water.

Fadis angled his bow, loosing into the dwarves one after another as they attempted to board. Braei sat on the deck, hyperventilating but trying to still look over the railings and cast whatever she could.

Valrin had his plan. He was new to sailing, but this was his ship. Ordained to him by birth in a storm upon the sea that cast him into the care of his aunt, Tua. He had taken the step forward in faith, and now he had to save the one who had done so much for him in the short time he was in his life. He had to save Edanos.

As he ran his ship beside the dwarven vessels, he twisted the crystals, sending blasts of arcane fire toward the ships. The dwarves who had been manning the crossbows fell back to avoid the searing stream. As he went ship to ship, he noticed the blasts weakening, but he had still done catastrophic damage to the other vessels.

The other dwarven ships, including Rugag's, were closing on them.

"Fadis, retrieve our friends. Do what you can, please."

"I will do so, Captain!"

As they came along the last ship, Valrin spotted that Edanos was on the ground, but the first mate was still up, and though covered in blood, he had not stopped killing those of his kind. Fadis jumped to the enemy ship, and Valrin turned the wheel, forcing his ship into the dwarven one. The dwarves on the vessel had seen what had happened to the other ships and fled as Edanos and Rortho came aboard his ship. The mast of the *Truest Bliss* was still just visible, but the ship of Edanos was falling into the depths. That was not the fate of the remaining crew today. Fadis had retrieved Edanos, and Rortho followed.

"Valrin! Get us out of here! Toward OPEN sea this time!" Fadis shouted.

Valrin turned the ship away from the dwarven one and made for the open sea. As the other vessels of Rugag came near, he twisted the same crystal again and a blast of fire shot out again, this time toward the other vessels. The dwarven vessels did not pursue them and instead went to their other crippled ships. The had escaped and Valrin guided them into the bleak expanse. Safer waters, at least for now.

Fadis had taken the helm as Valrin went to Edanos.

"Vals, you should have left me. You were reckless. You could've gotten yourself and this ship destroyed."

He stared at him, seeing the anger in his eyes and the anguish of the pain he was in. He smiled. "Seems I need a captain to teach me still."

Edanos smiled back. "It does seem so."

Rortho knelt down, pushing a strange herbal mixture into the many wounds Edanos had. The bolt from the dwarven attackers was still in place.

"He will need healing, something beyond our skill set. We had supplies on the other ship, but this ship does not quite seem seaworthy beyond having some flashy powers, if you can call 'em that."

Valrin looked around. He did not yet understand the vessel they were on, but there had to be something. It was then a blast of water sprayed the deck. He went to the edge and noticed a whale pushing a wooden box.

As he tried to reach for it, he found it just out of reach. Rortho used his ax to pull it closer and then reached down to pull it out of the water.

The chest itself had the same emblem as the door before the place where they had gotten the ship. It was the image of Meredaas. He opened the chest to find several golden items, none of which he knew what were for.

There was a single parchment within, and it was addressed to Valrin directly.

He opened the letter and began to read.

Valrin, Stormborn. You have escaped from near death, saved one who believed in you, and now sail upon the seas of uncertainty. You have a vessel unlike any other, and you must learn it and unlock its true powers. There is much for you to discover, but I do say for you to take these devices I have included. Set them upon the aft deck and watch as the powers of the seafarers awaken. From there, you will be led in time to where you must go. There is much more for the Stormborn to do.

The message said nothing else. He carried the box to the rear of the ship and took the golden items. Each were a different prism. They were made of gold but were near opaque. He set each of them on the ship's deck, and they began to spin before floating together and moving into the wood itself. On the lower deck, a stone and metallic altar of sorts formed out of the very wood of the ship. A massive image of what Valrin could only describe as a floating map made of air appeared before them.

"A map of the sea," Fadis said. "I do not recognize most of this, but to the far south is where we met up, Merea. I can tell from the outline. But whatever this is, it is moving. Like it is the actual sea itself."

Valrin stared at the map, seeing a dense cloud cover moving over the image that matched the clouds above. As he stared, he saw an island. He turned the ship, and it seemed the map he stared at changed as well.

"We will try here," he told the others. He wasn't sure where they were going, but considering they were so far north and none of them knew where exactly to go, it seemed like the best idea. He did not know how much time Edanos had, and as his friend seemed to be breathing faster and in more pain, he assumed not too long at all.

In time, they came upon the island seen on the map. Though it was abandoned itself, Rortho was able to find supplies good enough to remove the barb from Edanos.

He started a fire and got a small knife red hot.

"This is going to hurt, but you know I must," the dwarf warned.

Edanos has fallen unconscious and was struggling to breathe. At the last moment, and to their surprise, a fairy floated down and moved over Edanos' wounds. Rortho quickly removed the barb. Edanos opened his eyes for a moment, and his breathing returned to normal. The fairy criss-crossed over his body and it seemed that after being healed by the power of the fairy, Edanos fell into a deep sleep.

They departed the island, sailing south for a time as Valrin tried to prepare for what it meant to be a Stormborn. The dwarves of Rugag were not going to simply allow him to escape, but he had beaten them once. In his young mind, for at least now, that was enough. The moon rose, and he did not feel tired as the others were. Though Fadis and Braei both questioned him, he gave them his reasoning, which they didn't believe but were too tired to argue.

As he glanced up at the night sky and millions of stars, the polar lights shined a bright green. He closed his eyes. He was Valrin of Travaa.

Stormborn.

His true quest had just begun.

Letter to Readers:

2019 Update:

The series is now nine books long with novel length works starting with book four! Thank you to all of you who have supported me through the years!

Hello!

If you're reading this it means you must have gotten to the end and decided to check out my little note to you. First off, how was the story? I know it wasn't as long as my other books but if you're wanting more I can at least assure you that the next book is a good bit longer. :)

So, this novella was something I had an idea for but wasn't too sure about at first. After a bit of discussion on my Facebook page and a small vote from a few of you, I decided just to jump right into it. I honestly intended for the story to just be one book. I actually killed two of the main characters in my original outline. . . but Valrin wouldn't have it. As it is right now the story continues for two more books. Book two is written. Book three is in progress. In this three book arc Valrin continues to come into his own destiny as the captain of the eventually named *Aela Sunrise.* (wait, should I of said "spoiler alert"? Hmm, well then. . .) It also sets a bit up for the big events of Half-Elf Chronicles but then it quickly diverts away from that. There is only so much that can be done at this time in Valrin's world in regards to those specific future events. But I do think you will have a lot of fun in these books.

There is a lot still to come in the Glacial Seas. Shadow elves, dwarven lichs, pet snakes. . . All the nice stuff! By the way, did you notice any easter eggs related to my other books? (maybe that small one about the elven swordsman who taught Valrin a bit about fighting?) If you didn't, keep watch for them in the next book. :)

Take care and I feel free to shoot me a message with any ideas or stuff you would like to know more about. I might include it in a future book!. ;)

J.T. Williams
Facebook: @fantasyauthorjtwilliams

ABOUT THE AUTHOR

USA TODAY BESTSELLING author J.T. Williams writes both epic fantasy, inspired by the likes of Tolkien, Salvatore, and Brooks, along with darker sword and sorcery, fueled by countless hours playing Elder Scrolls, The Legend of Zelda, and many other fantasy RPG/MMORPGs. When he isn't writing, he wages war in his backyard with his children having make-believe battles against the orcs invading from next door. He is married and has five little orc-slayers.

As a longtime lover of fantasy and the surreal, he hopes you enjoy his contributions to the world of fantasy and magic.

www.authorjtwilliams.com

Made in the USA
Monee, IL
15 September 2020

42567373R00059